WRITTEN BY CRYSTAL BOWMAN
ILLUSTRATED BY TERRY JULIEN

Scripture: [God] gives us everything to enjoy. 1 Timothy 6:17

Published by Standard Publishing, Cincinnati, Ohio
www.standardpub.com

ISBN: 978-0-7847-3603-6

Library of Congress Cataloging-in-Publication Data

Bowman, Crystal.
  The best thing about my birthday / written by Crystal Bowman ; illustrated by Terry Julien.
    p. cm.
  Summary: From the time she wakes up to a hug from Mama until her prayer of thanks at bedtime, Bunny enjoys spending her birthday with her family and friends.
  ISBN 978-0-7847-3603-6
  [1. Stories in rhyme. 2. Birthdays--Fiction. 3. Rabbits--Fiction.] I. Julien, Terry, ill. II. Title.
  PZ8.3.B6773Bes 2013
  [E]--dc23
                                                            2012030758

18 17 16 15 14 13   1 2 3 4 5 6 7 8 9

PUBLISHING
Cincinnati, Ohio

A hug from Mama is a very nice way
for Bunny to start her special day.

A yellow dress and a floppy hat—
Bunny decides she is happy with that.

A birthday breakfast just for Bunny—
carrot pancakes with butter and honey.

"Here are some cupcakes just for you.
Share with your friends and teacher too."

It's time for lunch. The school bell rings.
"Happy Birthday!" everyone sings.

Bunny likes sharing her birthday treats.
Carrot cupcakes are yummy to eat.

Bunny is home. The school day is done.
Grandma and Grandpa join in the fun.

Everyone sings a birthday song.
Little Bunny sings right along.

Birthday presents—three in a row.
Little Bunny pulls off a bow.

Wrapping paper falls to the floor.
Bunny gets to open one more.

Bunny says, "Thank you for my book.
Here, Little Bunny, you may look."

"Grandpa, please read my book to me."
Bunny sits on her grandpa's knee.

Bunny rubs her sleepy eyes.
But wait—she finds another surprise!

Bunny prays to God above,
"Thank you for birthdays filled with love."

Bunny tells Mama, "Birthdays are fun. The best part is sharing with everyone!"